Those Amazing Dinosaurs
and Other Prehistoric Animals

A Book of MAZES!

Written and illustrated by **John Cartwright**

Watermill Press

10 9 8 7 6 5 4 3

Brontosauru[s]

Brontosaurus means "thu[nder]
lizard." This plant-eater was seve[nty]-
five feet long and weighed thirty t[ons]

START

FIN[ISH]

Triceratops

...ceratops fed on plants and used
...three horns and tough, leathery
...n to protect itself.

START

FINISH

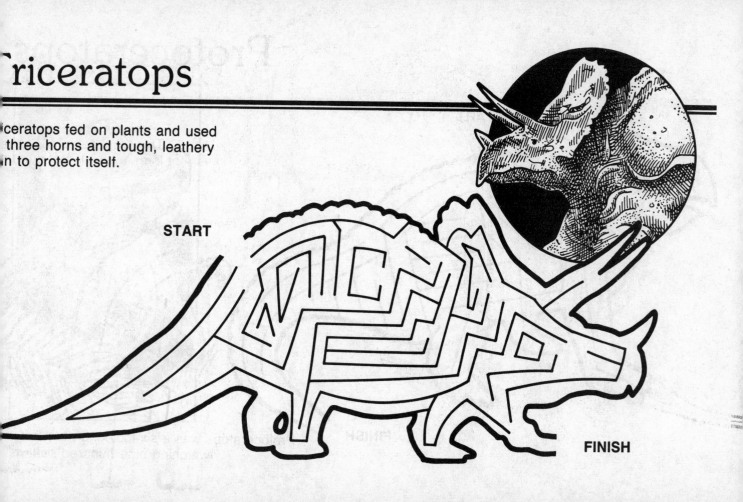

Protoceratops

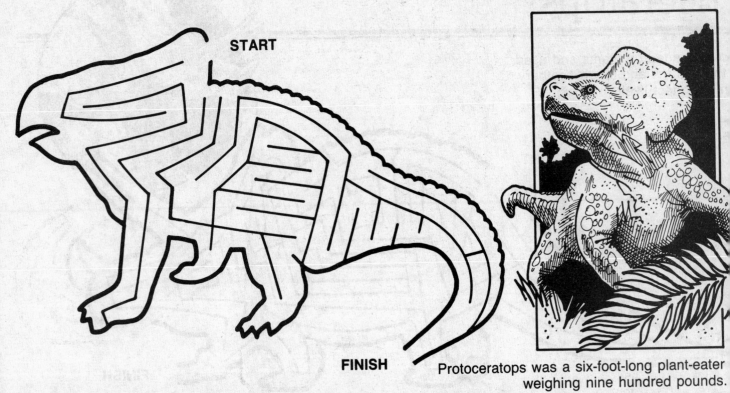

START

FINISH

Protoceratops was a six-foot-long plant-eater weighing nine hundred pounds.

Allosaurus

Allosaurus was thirty-six feet long and weighed approximately four tons.

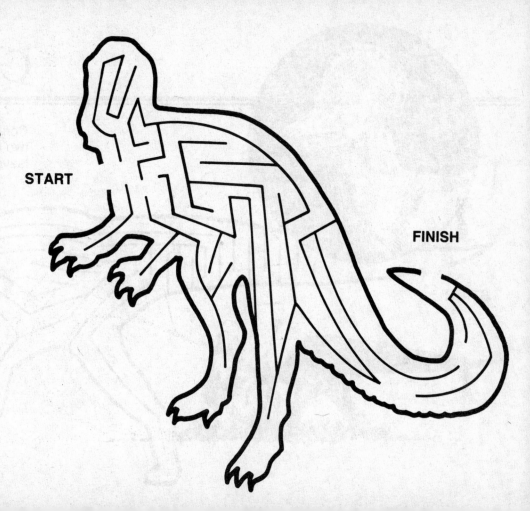

START

FINISH

Corythosauru

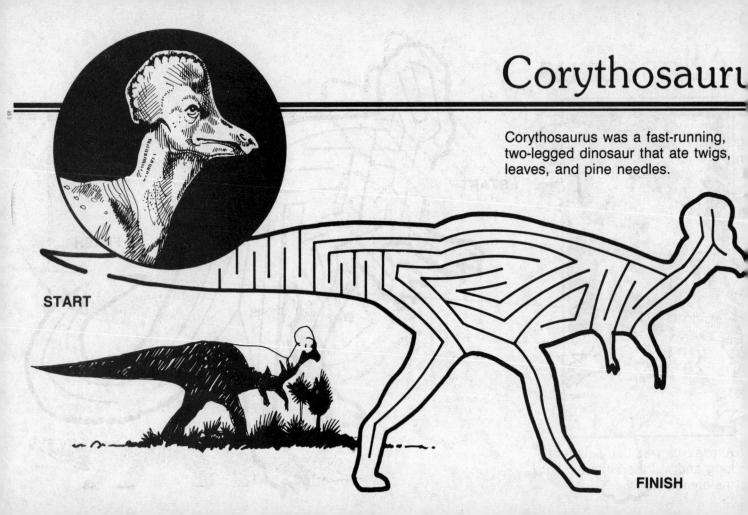

Corythosaurus was a fast-running, two-legged dinosaur that ate twigs, leaves, and pine needles.

START

FINISH

tegosaurus

gosaurus was
nty-five feet long
had a brain as
as a walnut.

START

FINISH

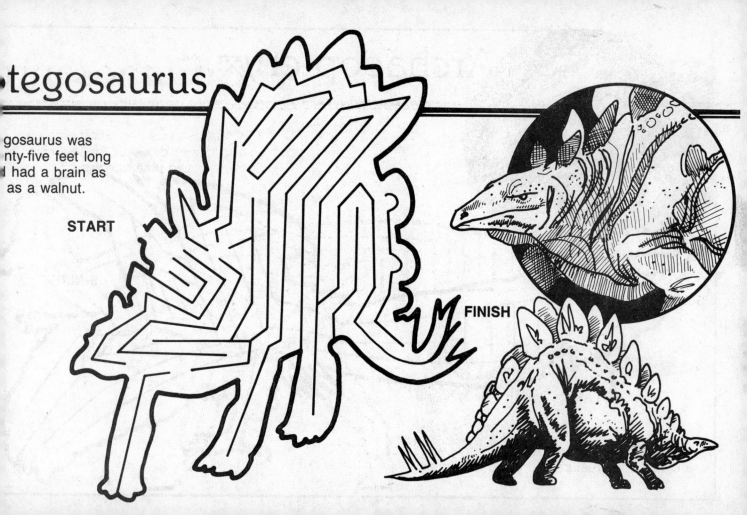

Archaeopteryx

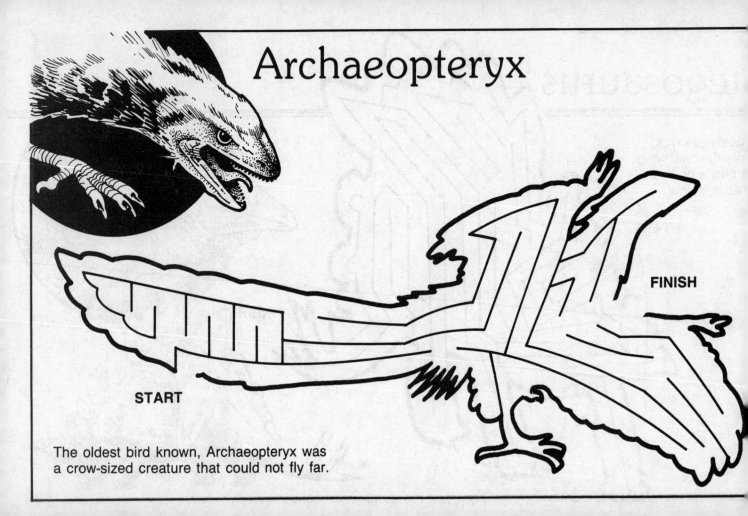

START

FINISH

The oldest bird known, Archaeopteryx was a crow-sized creature that could not fly far.

Chasmosaurus

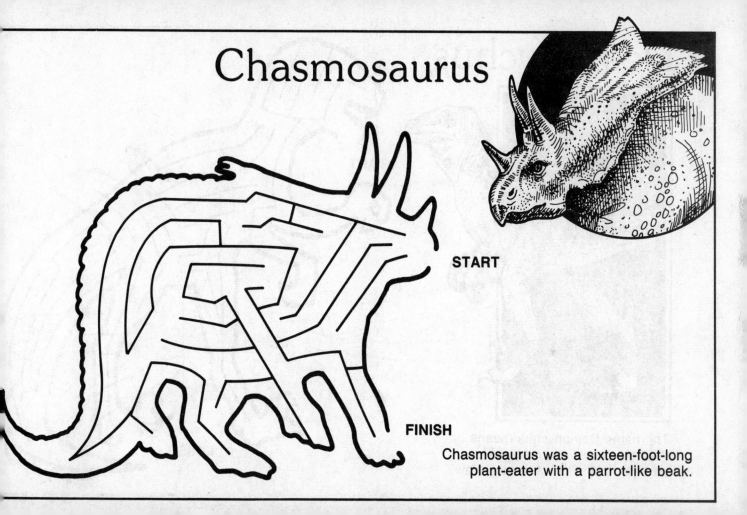

START

FINISH

Chasmosaurus was a sixteen-foot-long
plant-eater with a parrot-like beak.

Deinonychus

The name Deinonychus means "terrible claw." The second toe on each foot was a five-inch claw.

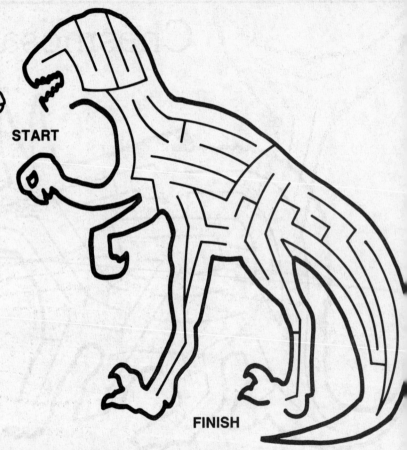

START

FINISH

Ichthyosaurus

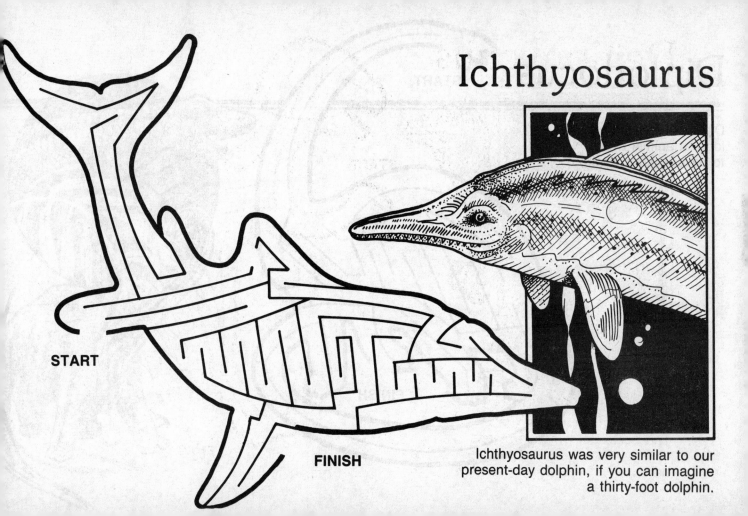

START

FINISH

Ichthyosaurus was very similar to our present-day dolphin, if you can imagine a thirty-foot dolphin.

Diplodocus

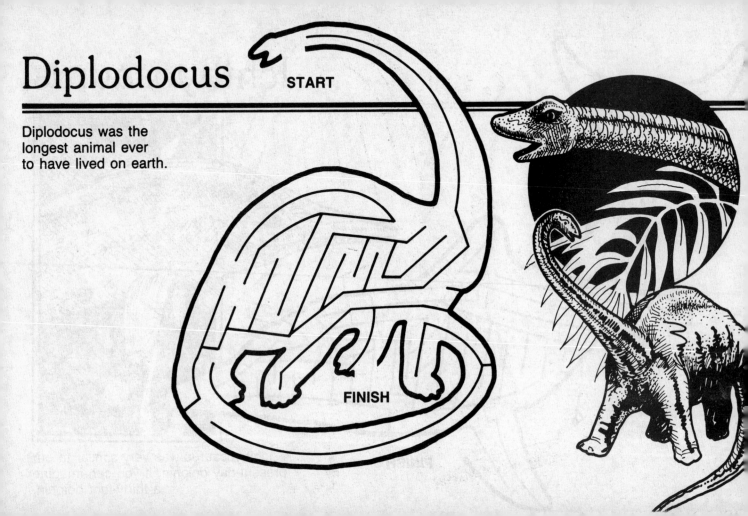

START

Diplodocus was the
longest animal ever
to have lived on earth.

FINISH

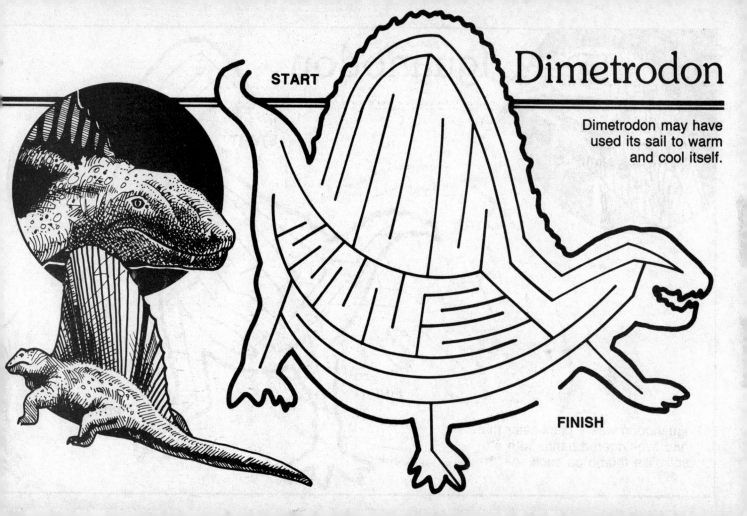

Dimetrodon

START

FINISH

Dimetrodon may have used its sail to warm and cool itself.

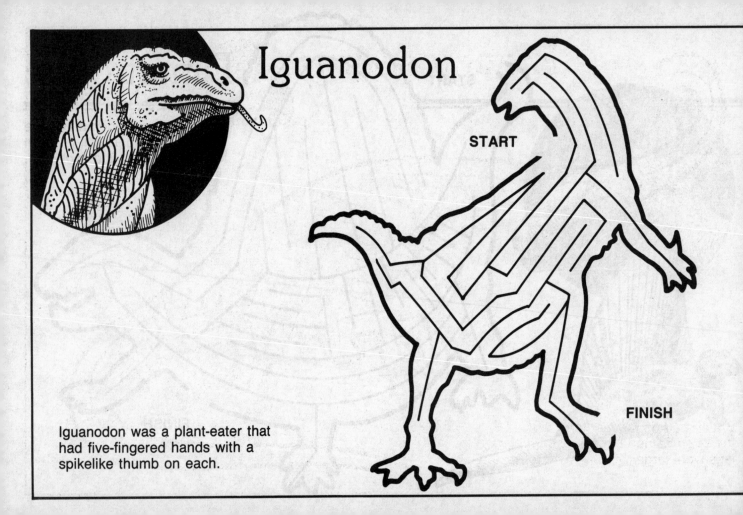

Iguanodon

START

FINISH

Iguanodon was a plant-eater that had five-fingered hands with a spikelike thumb on each.

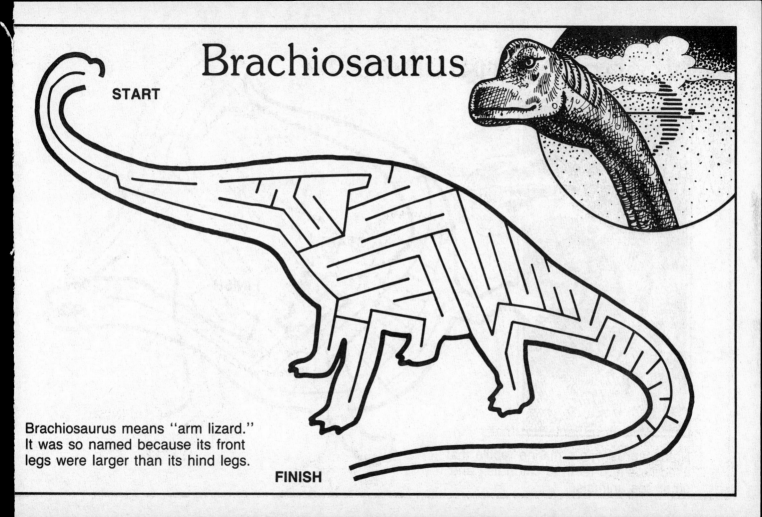

Brachiosaurus

START

FINISH

Brachiosaurus means "arm lizard."
It was so named because its front
legs were larger than its hind legs.

Nothosaurus

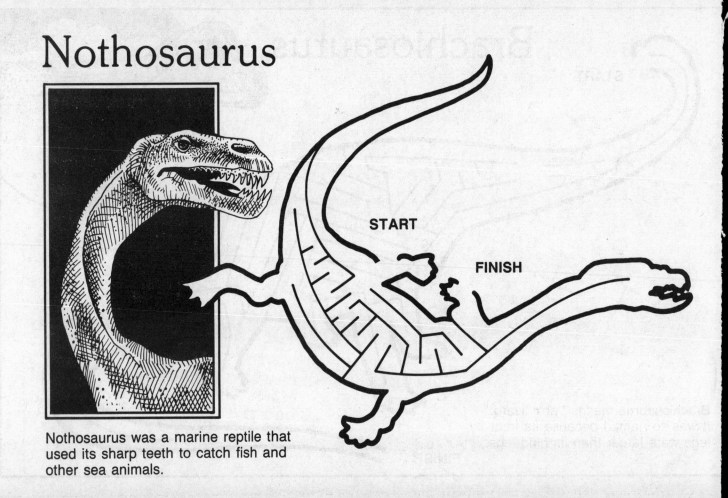

START

FINISH

Nothosaurus was a marine reptile that used its sharp teeth to catch fish and other sea animals.

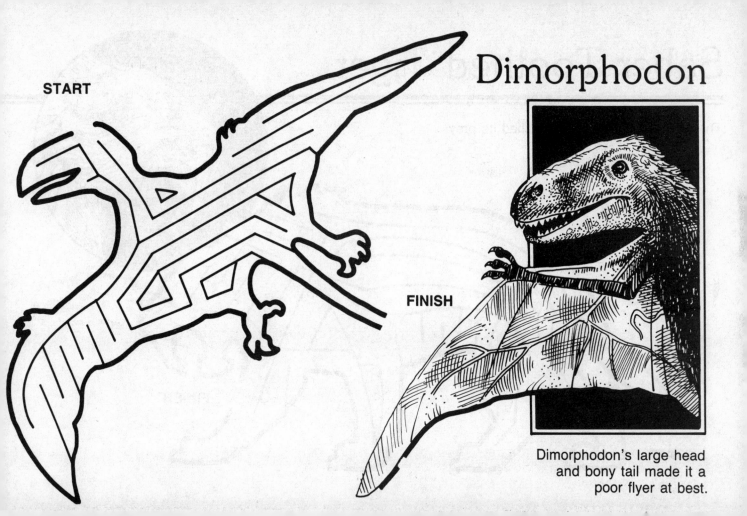

START

Dimorphodon

FINISH

Dimorphodon's large head
and bony tail made it a
poor flyer at best.

Saber-Toothed Tiger

The saber-toothed tiger ambushed its prey.

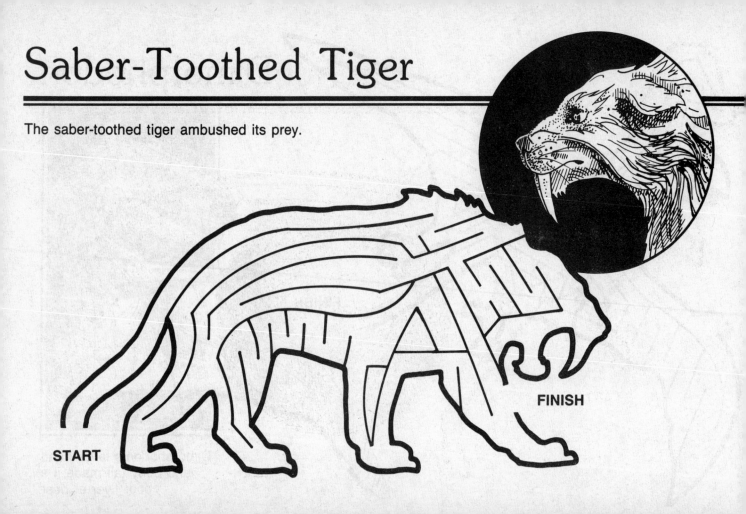

START

FINISH

Pachycephalosaurus

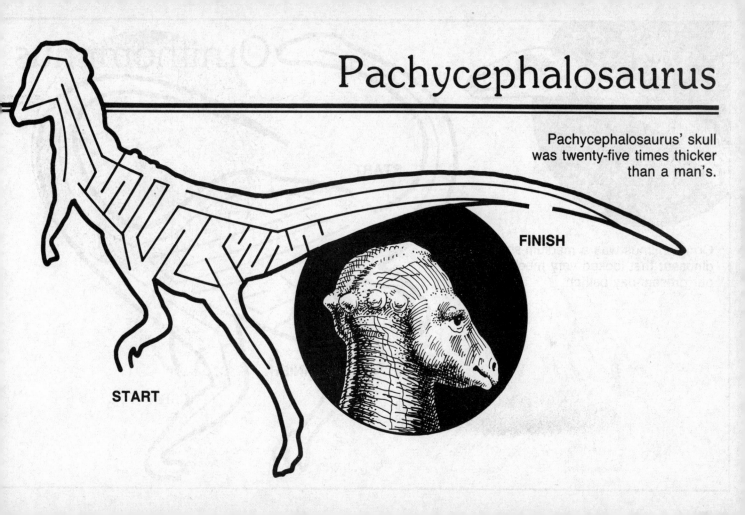

Pachycephalosaurus' skull was twenty-five times thicker than a man's.

FINISH

START

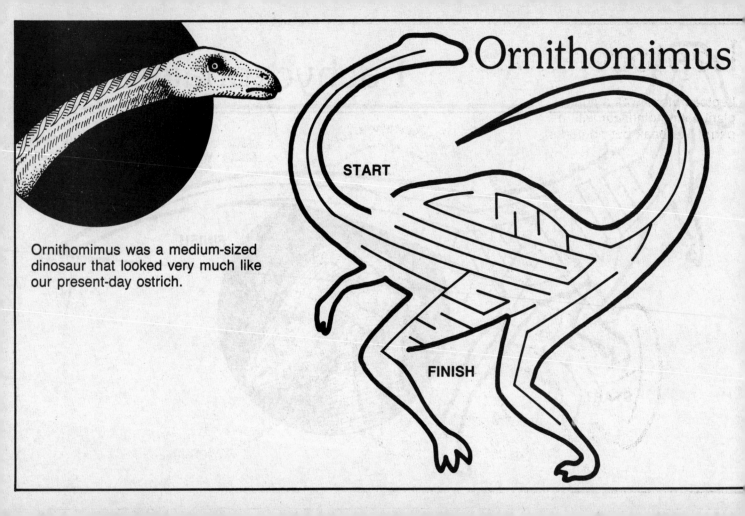

Ornithomimus

START

FINISH

Ornithomimus was a medium-sized dinosaur that looked very much like our present-day ostrich.

Leptoceratops

Leptoceratops was a small, plant-eating dinosaur with a parrot-like beak but no horns.

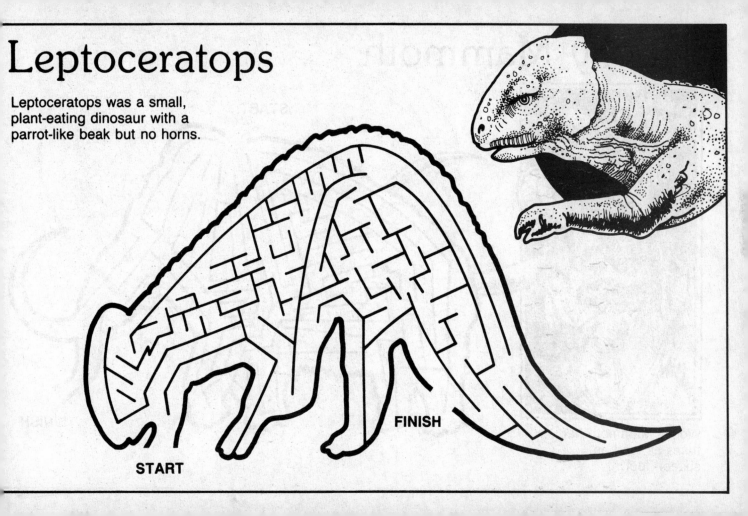

START

FINISH

Woolly Mammoth

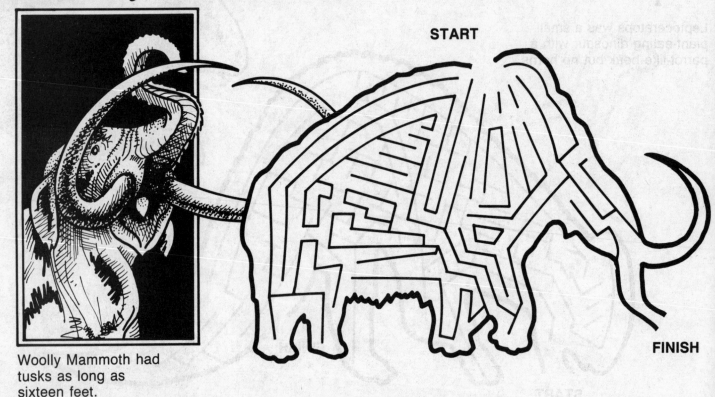

Woolly Mammoth had tusks as long as sixteen feet.

START

FINISH

Hypsilophodon

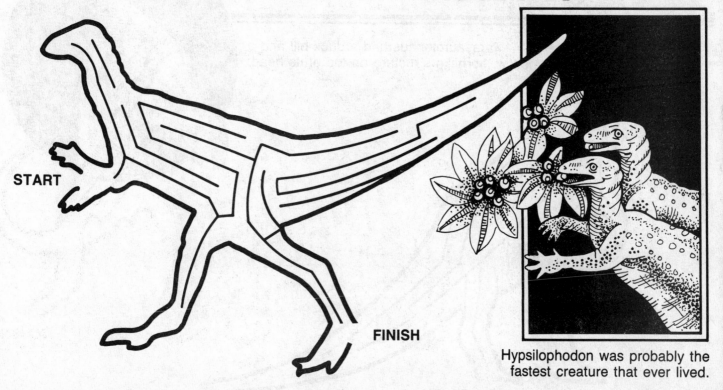

START

FINISH

Hypsilophodon was probably the fastest creature that ever lived.

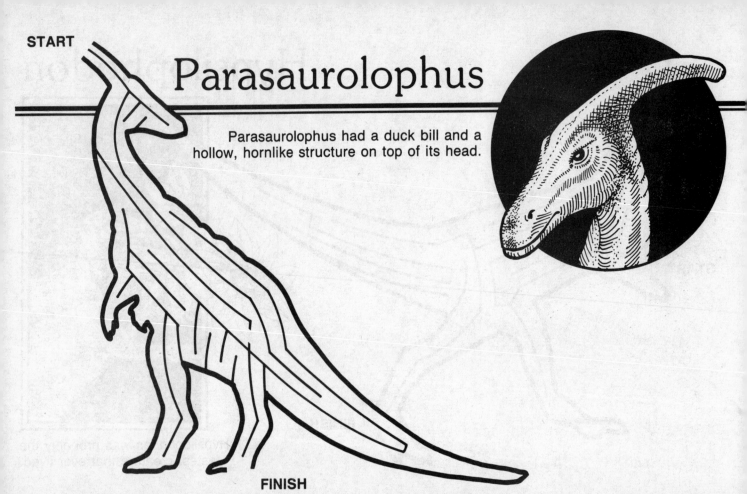

START

Parasaurolophus

Parasaurolophus had a duck bill and a
hollow, hornlike structure on top of its head.

FINISH

Basilosaurus

Basilosaurus was actually
an early form of whale.

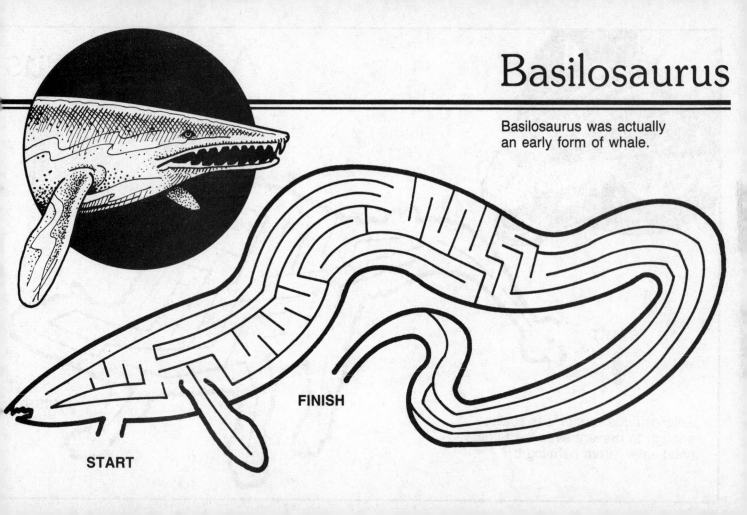

START

FINISH

Ankylosaurus

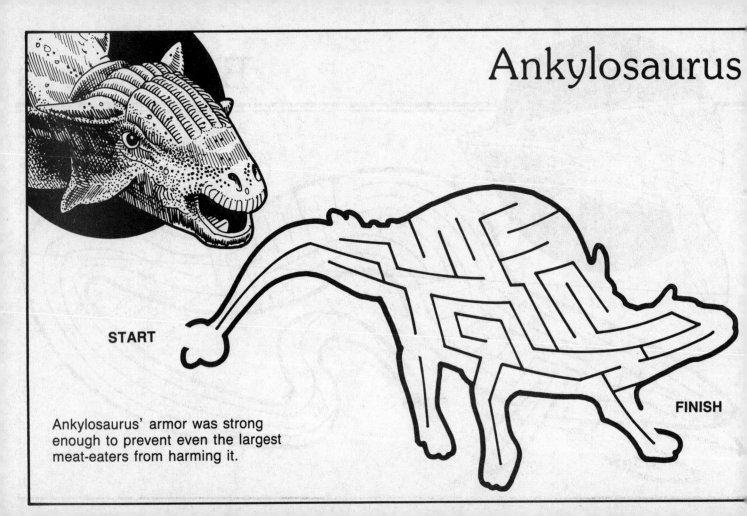

START

FINISH

Ankylosaurus' armor was strong
enough to prevent even the largest
meat-eaters from harming it.

Plesiosaurus

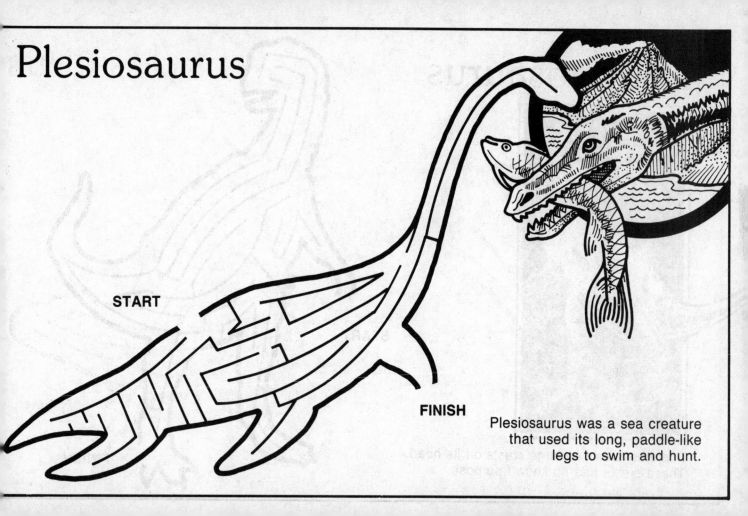

START

FINISH

Plesiosaurus was a sea creature that used its long, paddle-like legs to swim and hunt.

Dilophosaurus

Dilophosaurus had large crests on its head.
These crests had no known purpose.

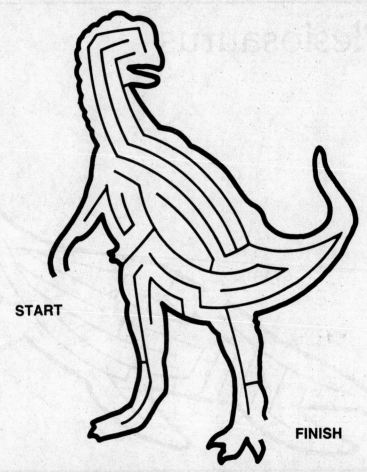

START

FINISH

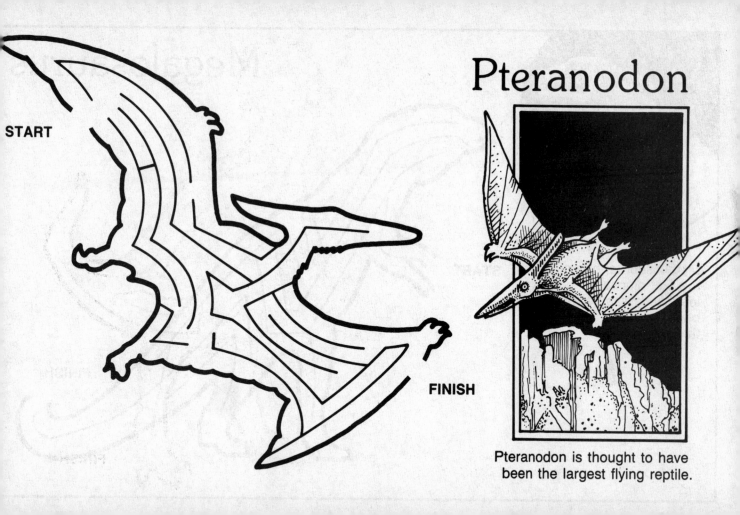

START

FINISH

Pteranodon

Pteranodon is thought to have been the largest flying reptile.

Megalosaurus

Megalosaurus, one of the first dinosaurs identified, was heavily built and had a short, thick neck.

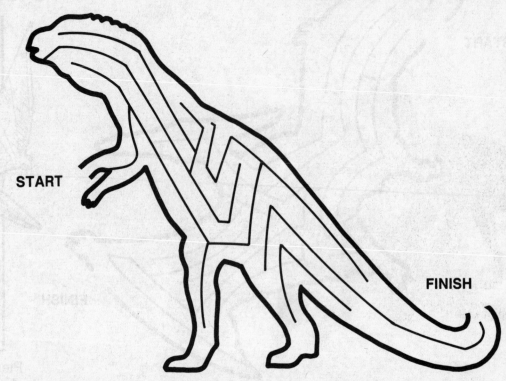

START

FINISH